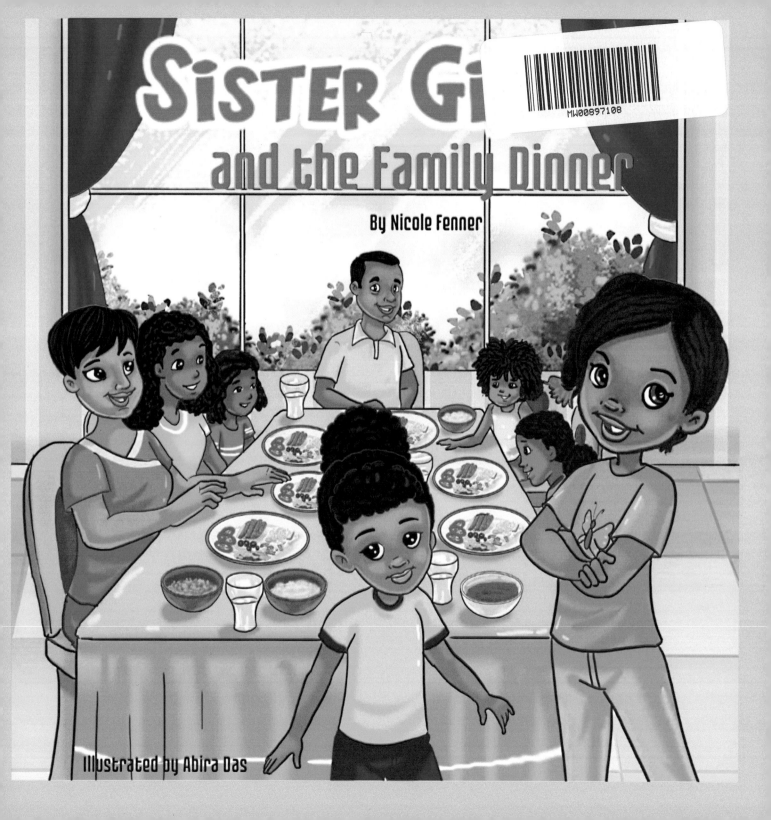

ISBN: 978-0-578-33840-8

Sister Girl Publishing PO Box 811, Halifax, NC 27839

info@sistergirlcollection.com
sistergirlcollection.com

DEDICATION

Sister Girl and the Family Dinner is dedicated to our families that light the torch and plot the course for the next generation. Your guiding light and unconditional love lighten our paths, even on the darkest days.

Momo, the delightful bright red cardinal, and Coco, the graceful blue jay, chirped sweet melodies as they flew around the puffy Carolina blue skies.

The forest green pecan trees swayed in the breeze while singing and laughter filled the brisk air.

Sister Girl and her sister Opal ran through the beautiful field of tall yellow sunflowers, as the summer sun shined down on their gorgeous sun-kissed skin.

Mom called out to the girls to come and help her water the family's blooming flower and seasonal herb garden.

Mom's flower garden was full of an amazing assortment of dreamy flowers. There were lovely rose bushes in an array of colors: red, lavender, rose pink, violet, and yellow. They smelled like a yummy sweet treat. There were also a rainbow of tulips, orange and yellow marigolds, bluebells, white kata lilies, warm buttercups, and pretty daisies.

Magical butterflies flew over Sister Girl's head while Opal and mom watered the seasonal herbal garden. Buzzing bees danced around and pollinated the light purple lavender, green mint, savory rosemary, and thyme. Mom made teas, soups, sauces, and scented oils with the herbs.

Perched on the branches of the pecan tree,
Momo and Coco looked over the flower garden.

Momo and Coco said to Sister Girl, "Let's go check on dad he is harvesting the vegetables in the garden."

Sister Girl and Opal skipped into the backyard, and there was dad. To their amazement, huge red tomatoes were hanging from the vines, sweet yellow corn, green bean hanging from the stalks, yellow squash, red potatoes, and delicious green and red peppers. The backyard was full of all the vegetables that you could imagine.

Over the last two months dad, mom, Opal and Sister Girl planted the seeds, watered the garden, and pulled out the weeds daily to cultivate the garden. This process helped the vegetables to grow big and healthy.

It was harvest time. The family harvested vegetables for the family's dinner. They harvested green beans, corn, peppers, potatoes, onions, cucumbers, and a handful of savory herbs from the herb garden filled with thyme, rosemary, lavender, and mint.

After harvesting the vegetables, Opal and Sister Girl played jump rope with their cousins Ruby, Amethyst, Emerald, and Sapphire while their cousins Jasper and Quartz played basketball with the neighborhood children.

Mom cut fresh flowers to decorate the house.
Mom placed fresh cut roses in the vase on
the kitchen table, breathtaking tulips
in the windows, and pretty daisies
in the living and dining room vases.
Mom's flower style was perfect.

Dad called out to the children that it was dinnertime. So Sister Girl, Ruby, Opal, Amethyst, Emerald, Jasper, and Sapphire came in for dinner. The cousins then washed up for dinner.

After they washed up Sister Girl, Opal, and their cousins helped mom set the dinner table, they placed the tablemats to match each chair at the table. Afterward, the children set the plates, napkins, glasses, forks, spoons, and knives in the right places on the table.

Everyone sat down for dinner, and all of a sudden, the doorbell rang right when mom was putting the food on the table. Dad looked out the window and he saw two afros. It was the Wunderkinds. Uncle Joe and Auntie June arrived just in time for dinner. They all hugged and sat down for the family's Sunday dinner.

Dad said a prayer of gratefulness for the family, the gardens, health, life, and strength. After prayer, the family ate their healthy and nutritious food. Dessert was fresh grapes from the grapevine, and a medley of peaches, pears, and apples from the family's orchard.

Sister Girl told her family that she was happy that she learned how to plant a garden, water the flowers, set the table for dinner, and to celebrate the wonders of the earth.

Momo and Coco watched the family from the bird feeder in the kitchen window and smiled at their awesome family.

Mom and dad told Sister Girl that everything you need in the world could be created, as long as you take the time to nurture it.

Sister GiRL COLLECTION

**Thank you for supporting
The Sister Girl Collection!**

To check out more books, visit
SisterGirlCollection.com
Follow us on Instagram and Tiktok
@sistergirlcollection
Email: info@sistergirlcollection.com

Made in the USA
Columbia, SC
03 June 2024

36426441R00018